Jane
and the
DRAGON

A Dragon's Tail

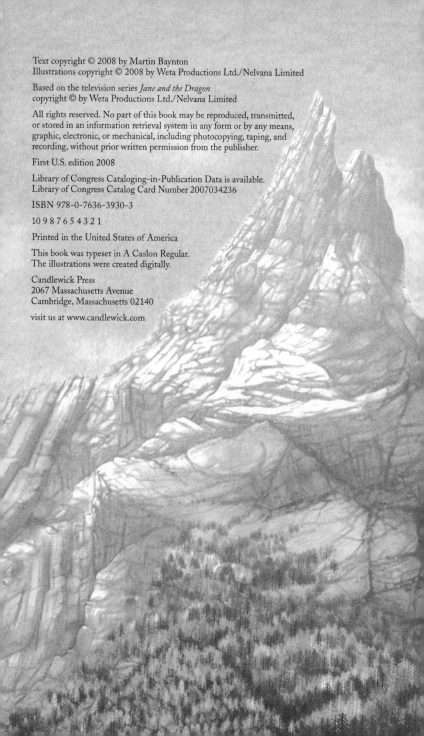

First U.S. edition 2008

Library of Congress Cataloging-in-Publication Data is available.
Library of Congress Catalog Card Number 2007034236

ISBN 978-0-7636-3930-3

10 9 8 7 6 5 4 3 2 1

Printed in the United States of America

This book was typeset in A Caslon Regular.
The illustrations were created digitally.

Candlewick Press
2067 Massachusetts Avenue
Cambridge, Massachusetts 02140

visit us at www.candlewick.com

Jane and the DRAGON

A Dragon's Tail

Martin Baynton

CANDLEWICK PRESS
CAMBRIDGE, MASSACHUSETTS

Cast of Characters

Jane

Brave and headstrong, Jane is determined to be the first female knight in the kingdom.

Gunther

A fellow knight-in-training who often disagrees with Jane

Rake

The Royal Gardener

Smithy

The Castle Blacksmith

Dragon
Jane's best friend

Pepper
The Royal Cook

Jester
The Royal Court Jester

The King
Cheerful and fun-loving

The Queen
Gentle, kind, and very beautifu

Princess Lavinia
Enjoys being a princess

The Prince
The Royal Brat!

Jane's Mother
Lady-in-Waiting to the Queen

Jane's Father
The King's Chancellor

Sir Theodore
Captain of the Guard

Ivon
A loyal knight

The Merchant
Rich and powerful;
Gunther's father

Chapter One

*J*ane was tiring fast. She had blisters on her sword hand, sweat in her eyes, and an elbow in her ribs.

A sword came arcing toward her. Jane dived, rolled, and sprang to her feet, ready to strike back. But a thump between her shoulders sent her sprawling to the ground.

"Maggots!" she snapped. "Weevil-bogging MAGGOTS!"

Jane and Squire Gunther were fighting back to back against their teachers, working as a team. But it was hard partnering with someone who kept knocking you over.

"The two of you must fight as one," said Sir Theodore. "Trust each other as you would trust your sword arm."

Jane hauled herself to her feet. She was bruised and VERY hungry. Weapons training always made her hungry.

"Sir Theodore," whined Gunther, "how can I trust someone who keeps elbowing me?"

"So keep clear of my elbows!" growled Jane as she made ready for the next attack. It came in a blur of wooden swords. Jane tried her best, but her teachers were good. Very good. In no time at all, Jane and Gunther were lying in a tangled heap on the floor.

"Very disappointing," sighed Sir Theodore.

"Jane tripped me!" snapped Gunther. "I fight better on my own!"

"Listen, boy," said Sir Ivon, "in the field you fight for your friends."

"And what if your friend is a cart horse?" asked Jane.

"Enough!" said Sir Theodore. "You will fight for each other as if your lives depend on it. As one day they will."

Jane was about to apologize when a long groan distracted her.

"Uuuurrrghhh!"

Dragon came swooping in over the castle and landed on the wall above them. He looked very green, even for a dragon.

Sir Theodore sighed. "You may attend to your friend, Jane." He knew better than to keep Jane from her dragon.

Jane thanked him and sprinted up the steps. "Are you all right?" she asked. "You look as bad as bog water."

"Well, hello to you, too," groaned Dragon. He squeezed his eyes shut and sneezed. A jet of flame shot out and scorched the moss on the battlement wall.

"Dust," he grumbled. "Someone should sweep up around here. Really, what do you short-lives do all day?"

Jane wasn't fooled. She waited with her hands on her hips like a patient mother.

Dragon rolled his eyes. "Jane, I am fine. Thank you."

"You are NOT fine. Drop your head." Jane glared at him until he did what he was told. Then she reached out and put a hand to his forehead. It was damp and very hot.

"Dragon. You are SO hot."

"Why, thank you, kind lady."

"I mean it. You have a fever. Come down to the yard so we can check for symptoms." Dragon groaned and toppled off the wall. Jane glanced down at him. "Symptoms like a sudden bout of drama-queenitis."

Chapter Two

*J*ane was worried. What if Dragon was seriously ill? How could she help him? What could she do? And what sort of illnesses did a dragon get?

"Have you eaten anything strange today?"

"No, just the usual," he said. "Stinging nettles, bog myrtle. Some rotten mandrake root."

"Mmm, tasty," said Jane. "Let me get Smithy. He might have some ideas."

"Smithy?"

"Yes. He takes good care of the horses."

"Horses! Exactly! And do I look like a horse?"

"Only on a good day. Wait here." And she marched into the stables to find Smithy.

The young blacksmith listened patiently as Jane explained the problem.

"I can take a look at him, Jane. But I only know about horses. I can drain an abscess and comb for botflies."

"Just do your best, Smithy. And how different could Dragon be? They both have four legs, a head, and a tail."

"Yes, Jane, but wings?"

"Well said," yelled Dragon from outside in the yard.

"And both have VERY BIG EARS!" shouted Jane as she headed back out to her patient. Smithy was right behind her and set to work straightaway.

"I always look in the mouth and check the teeth first."

"Fangs!" said Dragon. "I have fangs, not teeth." But he opened his mouth all the same.

"The teeth, er, fangs, look fine to me," said Smithy, "but your throat looks a bit sore. Say *aaahhh*."

Dragon said, "Aaahhh," but it turned into a loud burp that sent Smithy reeling backward and gasping for air.

"Yuk! That smells NOTHING like horse breath!"

"You get used to it," said Jane.

Smithy gently took hold of one of Dragon's ears so he could look inside. Dragon pulled away.

"Watch it, hammer-boy! No one grabs the ears!"

"I need to see inside them," said Smithy. "Red and tender ears are a sign of fever."

"I have my dignity!" growled Dragon.

"Yes," said Jane, "AND a sickness of some kind. So let Smithy find out what it is." Dragon sighed and let Smithy peer into his ears and up his nose and listen to the beat of his heart.

"That is a BIG heart," said Smithy.

"Yes it is," agreed Jane, "big and very soft."

At last Smithy finished his inspection.

"Well," said Jane, "do you know what it is?"

"I do," said Smithy. "And horses never get it."

"HA!" shouted Dragon. "Told you! Horses and dragons, completely different."

"Yes," said Smithy. "I have only ever seen your illness once before—in a pig."

"In a pig?" Dragon stared at him.

"Yes," said Smithy.

"A pig, Smithy?" Jane was as surprised as Dragon. "Are you quite sure?"

"A PIG!" roared Dragon, completely outraged.

"See for yourselves," said Smithy. And he pointed to Dragon's tail. Dragon twisted around to look at his long, spiny tail. It had a strange curl to it, like a corkscrew.

"I think you have a bad case of Curly Tail," said Smithy.

Dragon glared at his tail. "Stop that! Stop it at once!" But his tail just continued to curl. Dragon tried to sneak around and grab it. But his tail followed behind him, just out of reach. Dragon made a lunge and started chasing his tail in a wide circle all around the yard.

"Is it serious?" asked Jane.

"What? Having Curly Tail, or Dragon thinking he can grab it if he runs fast enough?"

"Smithy! This is not a joke. What if Dragon is really ill? What can we do?"

At that moment two things happened: Dragon ran into a wall and

Rake came into the yard to see what all the noise was about.

"Is Dragon all right?" asked the young gardener.

"No," said Smithy. "He has Curly Tail."

"Oh, good," shouted Dragon. "Tell the whole world!"

Jane pulled her friends to one side so they could talk without Dragon hearing.

"What can we do, Smithy? Is there a treatment?"

"There is for a pig. But for Dragon, who knows?"

"What is it?" asked Jane. "We have to try."

"A plant called Skyleaf. You can boil

the leaves to make a broth. It tastes disgusting, but it will fix a pig right up."

"Skyleaf—good. Do you grow it in your garden, Rake?"

"No, it grows high up. You could try the far side of the mountain, over-looking the sea. Skyleaf likes the salt air."

"Thank you, Rake. The far side of the mountain it is—and not a word to

our green friend over there. The big lump will try to follow me and will just make himself sicker."

"Your secret is safe with us," said Smithy.

"Safe and sound," agreed Rake, "in our heads." He tapped the side of his head. "Where nobody can get inside and find out what the secret is."

"Who are you talking to?" asked Dragon. Rake looked around. Smithy was heading back into the stables, and Jane was halfway up the steps to her tower bedroom.

"My secret self," whispered Rake. And he hurried away to the safety of his garden.

Chapter Three

Jane took the steps to her room three at a time. Dragon was sick, and it was up to her to help him. Her mind was made up. She would make the trek up the mountain, find the Skyleaf, and hopefully be back in time for her afternoon duties. She raced into her tower room and opened the big wooden chest at the foot of her bed. Inside was her dragon blade, the sword she and Dragon had discovered in the tunnels below his cave. When she went on patrol with Dragon, she was happy to leave her weapons behind. Ten sharp claws were enough defense for anyone. But this adventure was different. She had to go in secret without Dragon to watch over her.

In one quick move, she swung the scabbard onto her back and fastened the straps across her chest and around her waist.

Jane headed for the castle's back exit. She wanted to slip out unseen and be back before anyone knew she was gone. She was almost to the gates when she noticed a tall figure pressed back in the shadows of the wall. She kept walking, but her hand reached over her shoulder to grip the handle of her dragon blade.

"Relax, Jane," said a familiar voice. Sir Theodore stepped out from the shadows. "Word travels quickly in this castle, young lady."

Jane acknowledged her teacher with
a polite dip of her head. "Sir Theodore.
I should have sought leave, but Dragon
is ill, and time is my enemy."

"I am not here to stop you, Jane.
You need a companion on this quest."

Jane beamed up at him. This was so
like Sir Theodore. He could be a hard
taskmaster, and then in the flip of a
coin he would be there to support her.

"Sire! I would be honored to travel with you."

"As would I with you, Jane. And yet I have someone else in mind to help you." He gestured back toward the Royal Gardens. Swaggering down the path toward them was a grumpy-looking Squire Gunther.

Jane stared at him, then turned to protest. But the old knight held up a hand to silence her.

"This is not open to discussion, Jane. You and Gunther will work together. Is that understood?"

"Yes, sir," said Jane, "but—"

"No *buts,* Jane. You will assist each other. That is a direct order."

Jane tried to keep her temper as

Gunther strode past them and out through the iron gates.

"Come on, Jane!" he crowed. "Step out! And keep those elbows to yourself!"

Jane felt ready to explode. She wanted to say something—wanted to put Gunther in his place. But at that moment a pitiful wail came floating over the wall from the castle yard. Jane knew at once that it was Dragon, and suddenly nothing mattered except making him well. Her petty squabbles with Gunther would not get in the way of her mission. She would come back with the Skyleaf plant, or she would not come back at all!

Up ahead, Gunther paused to call over his shoulder. "Are you coming, Jane?

Teamwork takes more than one squire, you know."

Jane swallowed her pride, and her reply, and hurried after him out through the iron gates of the castle.

Chapter Four

*T*he view was stunning. They were halfway up the mountain trail when Jane stopped to catch her breath. She knew that Gunther was as breathless as she was. She also knew that he would rather fall down dead from exhaustion than suggest a break. He could be as stubborn as a donkey sometimes.

"Look at that, Gunther!" The castle lay spread out beneath them like a toy from the royal nursery. They were too high up to see people moving around, yet Jane could just make out the big shape of Dragon lying in the yard.

"Poor Dragon," she sighed. "I hope the others are taking care of him."

Gunther turned and glared at her. "Poor dragon? I expect the big frog is glad to be rid of you for a day. You cling to him like a limpet."

"I do not! He comes and goes as he chooses. And he chooses to be with me most days."

"Whatever." Gunther started back up the path.

"I do not cling! He helps me, and I help him. Friends help each other."

"Well, climbing this mountain is not helping me," snapped Gunther. "This is all your fault, you and your elbows."

"*My* fault? You tripped ME!"

"Because you were in the way. You

are always in my way, Jane. You always have to be the best. You and that stupid lizard!" Gunther strode off before she had a chance to respond.

"Gunther!" But that was all she could think of to say. The strength of Gunther's anger stung.

She let him get a few strides ahead of her before she continued up the track. When he was in one of his moods, there was no point trying to make conversation. And conversation was a distraction she didn't need, anyway. All that mattered was to get the Skyleaf for poor Dragon. What Gunther felt about it was his problem, not hers.

Chapter Five

"LOOK OUT!" Rake and Smithy ducked as Dragon's tail swung past their heads. THWACK! It slapped down and struck the ground just a few feet away.

"Woohhh! That was close!" shouted Rake. "Now I know how the mice feel when Pepper takes a broom to them."

The two boys had been studying the way Dragon's tail moved, wondering how they might help to control it. Smithy had suggested splinting it with rope and timber to keep it straight. Then the tail had twisted violently and thrashed toward them like a giant green whip.

"Sorry," groaned Dragon. "It's got a mind of its own."

Smithy and Rake took a few steps back, well clear of the danger zone.

"How bad is he?" whispered Rake.

"Hard to tell," Smithy whispered back. "He could be very sick."

"Whispers, whispers, give you blisters!" groaned Dragon. "Speak up, or come close so I can hear you."

"Sorry," shouted Rake. But he kept his distance and turned back to Smithy. "So, what can we do?"

"Whatever we can," said Smithy. And both boys leaped backward again as the giant tail flicked out and slapped the ground.

"But whatever we do, we do it as far from that tail as we can get."

"Oh, I know," said Rake, his eyes lighting up. "Soup! Pepper makes us vegetable soup when we are sick."

"Soup sounds good," croaked Dragon.

"Yes, why not?" said Smithy. "Worth trying, at least."

"One barrow of vegetables coming up," said Rake, hurrying off to his garden to start digging.

"Go easy on the broccoli," shouted Dragon as Rake sprinted around him in a very wide circle.

Chapter Six

The wind bit through Jane's clothing as she followed Gunther up the mountain trail. The going had become harder. Not only was the track steeper this high up, but it had wound around to the seaward side of the mountain, where a cold salt mist added to their troubles.

"We should have brought horses with us," grumbled Gunther. They had been walking in complete silence for so long that his comment surprised Jane.

"Yes," said Jane, "horses would have been a good idea."

Gunther stopped and frowned at

her. "Agreeing with me, Jane? What is this? Have you caught a sickness from your dragon?"

Jane felt a smart reply forming on the tip of her tongue, but she swallowed it. Another argument with Gunther was not going to help Dragon.

They were well above the tree line now, up where the mountain was just a cracked finger of rock poking into the sky—gray, broken rock, worn by a million years of brutal winds. Up ahead of them the path cut through a gap in the face of the rock. It led into a sheltered plateau of flat ground.

"Look. Is that it?" Gunther pointed to a haze of blue dots clustered on the far wall. Jane shielded her eyes from the stinging wind.

"Skyleaf!" she yelled. "It has to be! Look how blue they are." Growing from a fissure in the wall ahead was a spray of beautiful blue flowers. Jane ran toward them. The little petals seemed to shine as bright and blue as the sky itself.

Then suddenly, the ground disappeared in front of her. Jane struggled to stop, her arms whirling for balance, her feet skidding at the very brink of a ravine that plunged down into a swirling white mist.

For one brief, terrifying moment, Jane felt herself teetering over the edge, carried forward by the speed of her run. Her sliding stop kicked small stones over the edge. She watched them tumble away from her like giant raindrops. And then she was steady on her feet again, braced like a warrior for the next threat.

Gunther stepped up beside her. It was a long while before either of them could speak. They just stood together, staring down into the ravine.

Chapter Seven

*R*ake and Pepper hurried into the
yard. They carried baskets piled high
with vegetables from Rake's garden.
They approached Dragon slowly,
fearing his wayward tail might thrash
out and pulp them.

"The poor pumpkin," whispered
Pepper. "He looks worse than ever."

"Here we are, Dragon," said Rake.
"Vegetables for your soup. I dug them
from the garden myself."

"No broccoli, I hope," said Dragon,
opening one eye and peering at the
baskets.

"No," Rake replied, laughing, "no

broccoli. Mind you, I think it is a prince among vegetables. Did you know that broccoli is good for your skin?" He looked up at Dragon's scaly skin. "Perhaps if you ate more broccoli, your—" He jumped back as Dragon's tail slammed the ground at his feet.

"I meant that one," growled Dragon.

"Rake is only trying to help," said Pepper. "He promised Jane he would look after you. He dug up half his

garden to get these for your soup, so you have no business being cross with him."

Dragon sighed and reached out with his front paws to pull his tail in.

"So, where is Jane? She should be looking after me, not you. Is she helping you in the kitchen?" Pepper glanced sideways at Rake and shook her head.

"No, Dragon. Jane is on an errand."

"An errand? Who for?"

"For Theodore. She will be back shortly, and I dare say she will feed you the soup herself."

"Well, I suppose I could manage a little soup." Dragon sniffed the baskets, and the long fronds of a carrot top tickled his nose. Rake watched in horror as Dragon's giant green nostrils twitched and started to curl. He dropped his basket and grabbed Pepper, pulling her aside as Dragon roared a sneeze of orange flame.

Pepper got to her feet, thanked Rake for his kindness, and dusted herself off. Then she stared at the baskets of vegetables.

"If you wanted them roasted, you only had to ask," she said, and she hurried back to her kitchen.

Rake collected up the charred vegetables. "Roasted vegetable soup, coming up," he said. "Just what you need, Dragon."

"Listen, gardener," growled Dragon softly. "What I need is my good friend, Jane."

"Yes. Jane. Of course." Rake nodded his head furiously like one of Jester's wooden puppets. "Quite right. No doubt she will be back soon . . . er . . . from the errand for . . . for Sir Theodore." Rake beamed, pleased to have remembered Pepper's white lie correctly.

"How could she go off at a time like this?" whined Dragon. "My sides ache, my ears itch, and my tail . . . look at my tail. Look at it!" Dragon scowled at his tail. "Stop that twitchy, curly, thrashy stuff! STOP IT!"

"I wish I could do more to help," said Rake.

"You can," said Dragon. "You can go and find Jane."

Chapter Eight

*J*ane's heart slowed to a more sensible beat.

"Thank you," she said at last.

"For what?" asked Gunther.

"For not gloating. I broke the rules."

"Which rule?" Gunther turned to her, a slight smile on his face. "You mean the one about never charging until you know the lay of the battle-ground?"

"Yes."

"Or the one about consulting your fellow knights?"

"Both of them, I guess."

"Or the one—"

"All right!" Jane turned on him. "I broke every rule in the book. Satisfied?"

"Not yet." Gunther grinned and turned to leave. "But I will be when I make a full report to Sir Theodore."

Jane grabbed his elbow and turned him back to face her. "Fine, good. You make your report when we get back. But first we have a job to do, remember?" She pointed to the blue flowers growing on the far side of the ravine. Gunther looked at the plant and back at Jane.

"No way! That plant is sitting on a narrow ledge on the other side of . . . of nothing! Look at that drop, Jane. You could fall for a year before you hit the bottom!"

"Gunther, that plant is only three paces away."

"Three paces of thin air, Jane. It might as well be three leagues."

Jane spun away from him. He was right, of course, and she knew it.

"Pignuts!" she snapped. "Bog-rotten pignuts!" And she kicked a stone off the edge and watched it disappear down into the mist. "There has to be a way, Gunther. Dragon needs that Skyleaf. I have to get it for him." And she began to pace up and down in front of the drop, staring down at the mist and then across at the plant.

"We could jump it," she said. "I know we could."

"We!" Gunther said with a bitter laugh. "Jump that? What do you keep under that red hair? Compost?"

"Two strides, Gunther. And the far ledge is lower than the ground on this side. Look." She pointed to the narrow ledge where the Skyleaf plant was growing.

"Yes," said Gunther. "So even if we made the jump across without ending up as fish meal, we could never jump back again."

"There must be *something* we can do."

"We could cut your hair and make some rope."

"Funny!" Jane glared at him, then continued to pace back and forth. "This is serious. Think!"

"The last time I checked, neither of us could fly. Not without a lizard! So, unless you plan to grow wings, we should head back to the castle for a ladder."

"No." Jane shook her head. "That will take forever. There must be another way." She crossed to a small dead tree that lay twisted and broken against the rock face behind them.

The branches were too soft and rotten to make a bridge, but they gave Jane an idea.

She snapped free a thin branch, about the length of her arm. Then she drew her sword from its scabbard and split the end of the stick.

"There. I can pinch the plant into the end of the stick and pass it back to you."

"Pass it back?" Gunther couldn't believe his ears. "No, Jane, you are NOT going to jump across there."

"Yes, I am, unless you have a better plan . . . ?"

"I told you—a ladder. We go back and we—"

"No. Too slow." Jane held the branch like a lance and began to pace her run to the edge of the ravine.

"Ten steps and then jump. Plenty of room to get my speed up."

Chapter Nine

*G*unther stared in disbelief as Jane paced out her run.

"No, Jane. No way! This is not your decision. This is about teamwork, remember? So we discuss this AS A TEAM!"

"Then perhaps my team can wish me luck and keep out of my way." Jane had made up her mind and nothing was going to stop her—not Gunther, and not some vague promise to Sir Theodore. She hadn't asked for anyone's help. She had come to find a plant to help Dragon. Nothing else mattered. She stared at Gunther. She willed him

to step aside and let her do her duty to her friend. And he did. With a shake of his head, Gunther stood off to one side.

"Just . . . just try to be careful. Imagine what Dragon will do to me if I go back alone."

But Jane wasn't listening. Her training had taken over. She could hear Sir Theodore's voice in her head.

"Picture the moment of triumph, Jane. Picture success, never failure. Doubt is your greatest enemy." And with those words spurring her on, Jane dropped her head and charged toward the ravine.

It was only twenty strides, but it seemed to take forever. Jane hit the lip of the ravine with her right foot and pushed off into the air. As her speed took her sailing across the gap, Jane kept her eyes fixed on the plant on the opposite ledge. She had commanded herself not to glance down, not even for an instant. And her resolve held. She cleared the gap with ease and slammed down right on target in the middle of the ledge.

"Good," Jane said to herself, "very good." She jumped to her feet and turned in triumph to Gunther. But he was standing as tense as a longbow, his eyes squeezed shut.

"You can open your eyes now, Gunther." The remark was unfair, and she knew it. The relief on Gunther's face when he looked across at her was so great it was almost embarrassing.

"You jump like a frog," he said.

"So you were watching."

"Half of one eye," he laughed. "Just in case."

"I told you, Gunther. A simple jump, nothing to worry about. I had plenty of—" But Jane never finished her sentence. Without warning, there was a loud clap like the cracking of a giant whip, and part of the ledge fell away beneath her feet. It tumbled down into the ravine, taking Jane with it.

Chapter Ten

"JANE!" screamed Gunther. He ran forward and stared down into the throat of the ravine. Pieces of rock were still tumbling end over end into the mist. But Jane wasn't falling with them. She was clinging to the rock face on the far wall, hanging there like a fly, her fingertips gripping a thin wedge of jutting rock.

For a moment she was too stunned to think. She had reacted on instinct when the rock gave way. In a single movement she had turned and leaped for the back of the ledge, kicking off against the falling platform of rock.

And now here she was, clinging like a bat, taking shallow breaths so that her chest wouldn't push her loose.

As the shock passed, a sense of creeping dread set in. She could hear Gunther shouting to her, but her brain couldn't focus on the words. Her whole world had shrunk to the small piece of rock wall she was clinging to.

"Never panic." At first Jane wondered who was talking to her. Then she realized it was her own voice. Some quiet part of her was taking control. "Fear is your enemy," she whispered. "Never submit to fear." And suddenly a strange calm came over her. She felt the weight of her body pulling on her fingertips, and she knew she must find a foothold very soon before the strength in her arms gave out.

And then she heard Gunther's voice. He had been calling to her the whole time, but it had just been a noise in the background. A distraction. Now his words made perfect sense.

"A little to your left, Jane. Listen to

me. There's a foothold there. To your left, Jane."

Carefully she eased her foot out, scraping it up and down the rock face until she felt a slight bump.

She pushed down with her toe. The rock held. The relief on her aching fingers was immediate as the weight of her body was shared a little more kindly.

With her face pressed against the rock, Jane listened carefully to Gunther's instructions as he guided her back up to the safety of the ledge.

Chapter Eleven

The climb seemed to take forever, but at last she pulled herself over the lip and crawled back onto what little remained of the rock ledge.

"That was interesting," she said when she had her breath back.

"Yes," sighed Gunther. "Like having a tooth pulled. Exactly the kind of excitement I can do without."

"Sorry."

"Me, too, Jane. Sorry I agreed to come on this quest. Sorry I let you make that stupid jump. And most of all, sorry that no one was here to witness how completely I saved your irritating hide from being a big, flat mess on the rocks below."

"My hero," said Jane.

"Exactly. So be sure and tell that to everyone when we get back. Now, do NOT move. Not one inch while I go for help." Gunther turned to leave, but Jane called him back.

"Gunther! Wait! Take the Skyleaf with you!" She reached behind her and pulled the plant from the rock fissure where it had sent down its long, spidery roots.

"All right," sighed Gunther. "Throw it across. I might as well return a complete hero."

"Throw it? No, it might blow away in the wind. Why do you think I brought the stick?" Jane bent and picked up the stick she had dropped when she had first jumped across. Carefully she pushed the plant into the split she had cut in the end.

"Get ready," she said. "You may need to stretch for it." Gunther stepped as close to the edge as he dared and held out his arm. But he couldn't reach the plant.

"Lean out for it," said Jane. Gunther shook his head in disbelief and got down on all fours.

"No, Jane. Step one in helping your dragon is for me to run back with the plant. Not fly back with it." Jane watched as Gunther lay flat on his belly and wriggled to the edge to

extend his reach. Then, taking care not to look down, Jane reached out as far as she could with the branch.

"Got it!" yelled Gunther. And, grabbing the Skyleaf, he pushed back and stood up. A flood of relief washed over Jane.

"Take it to Smithy," she said, sitting back against the rock behind her.

Gunther clenched the plant in his fist and hesitated.

"Jane! Are you sure? Will you be all right?"

Jane nodded, though her voice betrayed her. "Yes. Go quickly! Bring Sir Theodore and some rope."

"And no moving, Jane."

"Not so much as a toe, I promise."

And with one last backward glance, Gunther was gone, racing off down the mountain trail.

Jane was alone—just one small girl perched high up a mountain on a narrow, broken ledge. She had been hugging her knees to her chest to stop them from shaking. Now, with no one left to see her, she could let go at last.

Her whole body began to shake with the fear she had bottled up since making the jump. And the young knight-in-training gave in to her private tears.

Chapter Twelve

CRASH. Dragon's tail thrashed about like a beached fish as Rake and Jester looked on. Dragon looked terrible. His eyes were closed, and a cold sweat had broken out over his body.

"More soup?" Smithy arrived, wheeling a large cauldron of soup on his barrow.

Dragon opened one eye and nodded. "If you insist." And he drained the cauldron in a single slurp. Rake leaned close to Jester and whispered in his ear.

"That is his fifth bowl! My garden

will be stripped bare at this rate. And poor Pepper has run her feet off cooking for him!"

"Where is Jane?" groaned Dragon.

"He keeps calling for her," whispered Rake. "I promised Jane we would keep him quiet. I keep telling stories to stop him from following her."

"Now, that I can help with," said Jester. "I draw the line at thrashing tails and flaming tonsils. But deception and sleight of hand . . . that's my job."

A few moments later, Jester was calling down to Dragon from Jane's tower room.

"Dragon. Oh, Dragon!" Jester was a clever mimic, and he called out in Jane's voice.

Dragon half opened his eyes. "Jane? Is that you?"

"Yes, Dragon," said Jester, and he waved the mop around. "Up here, in the window. Now, you lie still and let Smithy take care of you."

"All right, if you tell me to, Jane. Did you finish your errand for Theodore?"

Jester frowned. Rake hadn't told him about an errand.

"Er . . . yes. Of course."

"What was it, Jane? What did you get for old Rusty Legs?"

"Oh, er, you know. The usual. He wanted . . . er . . . a mirror . . . er . . . a mirror from the market . . . for his mustache. That was it . . . yes, a mustache mirror."

Jester repeated the last words quietly to himself in sheer disbelief at his own stupidity. Then the ground shook as Dragon thumped his tail down, and the mop tumbled from the window to land at Dragon's feet.

Jester managed a nervous laugh before hurrying down to face the music, his friends, and a very angry Dragon.

Chapter Thirteen

"*I* shall ask you one last time." Dragon pulled himself to his feet and glowered at Jester. Rake and Smithy stood shoulder to shoulder with him, prepared to share the blame.

"We were just trying to do what's best," said Jester.

"With lies and deception? Where is she?"

"Jane said not to tell you," stammered Rake. "She was afraid you might try to follow her and get even worse." Rake looked ready to faint and was glad to see Pepper hurrying into the yard to support them.

"Jane will be cross if we tell you," said Pepper.

"And you will be charcoal if you do not!" growled Dragon.

"Good point," yelped Jester. "Excellent. I vote for honesty and trust and a complete unburdening of everything we know." The four friends looked at each other and nodded.

"She went up the mountain," said

Smithy. "She went to find a plant to make you well."

Dragon's eyes narrowed. "Where on the mountain?"

"The far side," said Rake. "Up where the air is salty from the sea breeze."

Dragon snarled and shook his head. "The rock is weak and broken on the far side." And with a mighty effort, he stretched out his wings, beat the air, and lifted slowly and painfully from the ground.

"Wait!" shouted Pepper. But it was no good, and they all knew it. Nothing would keep Dragon from going in search of his friend. In just a few minutes, he was clear of the castle walls and heading for the mountain.

At that moment an exhausted Gunther came running into the yard. He was out of breath and clutching the Skyleaf plant.

"I have it! I have the plant for . . ." Gunther stopped and looked around the yard. "Where is Dragon?"

"Gone," said Pepper. "And where is Jane?"

Chapter Fourteen

*J*ane was trying not to panic. Fear
was bottled like vinegar in her stomach.
Sitting still on a tiny ledge, perched
high above a dizzy drop, was hard
enough. But ever since Gunther had
left, the rock had been groaning quietly,
as if the pressure of holding her up
were growing too much for it.

She tried not to listen. She thought
about the songs Jester sang in the
banquet hall and tried to remember
one so that she could sing it aloud.

And then she heard something else.
Above the creaks and groans of the
rock, above the distant crash of the

surf, she heard her name. It was faint, no more than a whisper, but she knew at once who it was.

"Dragon!" she yelled. "Dragon, where are you?"

With the rock walls rising up on either side, she could see only a small corridor of sky. And suddenly there he was, a distant green shape weaving through the clouds.

"DRAGON! DOWN HERE! DOWN HERE." She stood up carefully and waved. Then he spotted her. He turned and dived toward her, his tail twisting from side to side, his wings beating hard to keep his flight even. Jane grinned, then stopped and put her hand to her mouth. Dragon was falling.

"Pull up!" Jane screamed. "PULL UP!" But it was no use. He was sick and exhausted, and the flight had been too much for him. For one agonizing moment, Jane thought he was going to fall straight down into the ravine. Instead, he landed with a sickening thud just across from her.

The ground shook from the force of

the blow. Jane was thrown from her feet, and another chunk of her small ledge broke away and tumbled from sight.

"DRAGON!" screamed Jane. "Dragon, wake up. Wake up!" For a moment she thought he was dead. The fear that had been churning in her stomach rose up to burn in her throat. And then she saw the gentle rise and fall of his great chest, and she burst into tears again from the sheer joy and relief of it.

Chapter Fifteen

*C*rack! Jane felt the ledge tremble beneath her feet. Dragon's crash had pushed the fragile rock to the breaking point. In desperation she screamed out.

"Dragon, wake up! PLEASE."

But there was no response, just the rhythmic rise and fall of his chest and the mad swishing of his tail.

Dragon had crashed with his tail hanging down over the edge of the ravine. It whipped back and forth through the air in front of Jane, and for one mad moment she had an urge to leap out and grab hold of it. She knew at once that it was a stupid thing even to consider, and yet what choice did she have? She began to count the swings, timing the tail as it swept past her.

And then the decision was made for her. The ledge shuddered violently beneath her feet.

"Time to go," said Jane. And as the ledge crumbled away, she launched herself at Dragon's tail. For one long moment she was leaping through the air, then the tail slammed into her.

She hung on desperately as it slashed
through the mist, then she scrambled up
the ridge spines as if climbing a ladder.

She jumped down from his back
and ran around to peer into his eyes.
They were closed. She could tell at
once that he was in trouble. His skin
was cold and flaked with dry sweat.
His breathing was shallow, and a slight
wheeze rasped in the back of his nose.

Jane sat down beside him and rested her head against his cheek.

"Come on, Dragon. Hold on . . . please . . . stay with me . . . please, Dragon." She knew it was up to Gunther now. And she knew, in a way that she couldn't quite understand, that Gunther would come through for them. Despite all the anger, despite all the unkind words, Gunther was a fellow squire, a knight-in-training. And that meant more to him than winning some silly argument.

Chapter Sixteen

Jane didn't have long to wait.

"JANE!"

She looked up, and there was Gunther. He had arrived on horseback together with Theodore and enough rope and tools to rescue an entire army from the ledge.

"Did you bring it?" yelled Jane.

Gunther grinned and held out the Skyleaf plant.

"Yes. Plus a pot and tinder to boil it up. Smithy said to crush it first." With Theodore's help they collected dry branches from the broken tree and set the pot to boil over a small fire. When Jane was satisfied that the plant had cooked for long enough, she set the pot aside to cool and told Gunther of her leap onto Dragon's tail.

Gunther was wide-eyed with admiration. Sir Theodore shook his head and said nothing.

When the pot was cool to the touch, Gunther lifted it to Dragon's mouth and Jane began to stroke Dragon's throat.

"What are you doing that for?" asked Gunther.

"To make him swallow," said Jane. "Smithy does it to the horses." She pushed her shoulder under Dragon's head to help lift it and rubbed hard on his throat.

At first nothing happened. The contents of the pot emptied into Dragon's mouth and stayed there in the back of his throat. His breathing faltered, and

Jane rubbed harder on his throat. Then at last he swallowed, and coughed, and down went the medicine.

"Now we wait," said Sir Theodore.

The three of them sat and waited as the late afternoon sent long shadows stretching out across the ground.

Jane was almost asleep when she felt Dragon stir beside her. He opened his eyes and looked confused for a moment.

Then he saw Jane's happy face smiling at him.

"Hello," he said, then he screwed up his nose and starting spitting. "Ugggghhh! What is that disgusting taste! Yuuukkk!"

"Skyleaf," Jane said, laughing. "It tastes a bit like broccoli."

"Foul!" spluttered Dragon. "Completely, disgustingly, revoltingly foul."

"Maybe, but your tail seems to like it." Dragon turned to look at his tail. It was lying quietly behind him, not a curl to be seen.

"Come, Gunther," said Sir Theodore. "Let us get the horses back before dark. And Jane, I imagine you will be taking other transport, yes?"

"Yes, Sir Theodore."

"And well done, both of you. You showed excellent teamwork. Not quite the day I had imagined for you. But a lesson learned in the field stays with you forever."

Gunther and Sir Theodore set off down the track for their long ride back to the castle.

"Well, Lizard Lips," said Jane, when she and Dragon were finally alone, "no more getting sick on me. You had me very worried, you and your silly pigtail."

"I had YOU worried! The rock is very dangerous round here, Little Miss Stinky-Drink. What if that ledge had given way?"

"What ledge?"

"The one I saw you sitting on when I . . . er . . ." He stopped and stared at Jane. "It broke off!"

"But not before you saved me," said Jane.

"I saved you? I remember falling . . ."

"Your little curly pigtail saved me."

"It did?" Dragon reached around and picked up his tail and cradled it.

"Good tail," he said, and he stroked it like a kitten. "Good, brave tail."

"Come on," said Jane. "Do you feel strong enough to take me back?"

Dragon nodded, dropped his tail back behind him, and waited for Jane to climb up on his neck.

"Ready, Coppertop?" he said.

"Ready, Green Lips," said Jane. And away they went, two friends climbing up into the pink glow of an evening sky.

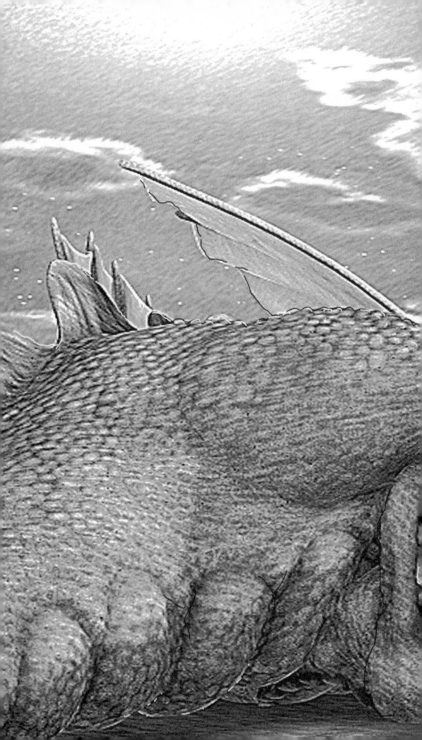

About the Author

MARTIN BAYNTON always wanted to be a writer and illustrator. At school, he used to get into trouble for drawing cartoons of his teachers, and his best grades were always for his story writing. Yet his first books weren't published until he was thirty. Up until then, he was too busy traveling the world and having adventures of his own. Martin lives with his wife on a small farm in Australia. They have two grown-up children, two dogs, and three horses. For the last four years, Martin has been working with Weta Productions in New Zealand, turning his *Jane and the Dragon* books into an award-winning television series.